Sally and Farmer Green stood back and looked at the farmer scarecrow they had made for the Village Scarecrow Festival. She was sitting on the old red tractor, which was parked at the top of the lane that went down to the farm.

The scarecrow was wearing some of Sally's old overalls, with a cap on her head and her arm was raised, as if waving.

Having decided that the scarecrow was finished, Sally and Farmer Green went home. They finished their jobs on the farm and then walked back down the lane and on to the village. They were going to go on the scarecrow trail around the village and see all of the other scarecrows that had been made.

Lots of visitors came to see the scarecrow trail and it raised funds for a local charity. The trail started at the village hall. There was quite a crowd there already, waiting to start.

Sally and Farmer Green paid for their map, which had all of the scarecrows marked on it, and set off. First, they walked across the square to scarecrow number one, outside the post office.

This scarecrow had a big hat with a sunflower on it, and a long flowery dress. She was holding a letter as if she were about to put it into the mailbox.

Next door at the garage, there was an old car with the hood up and some spanners and hammers next to it on the ground. There was also a pair of scarecrow's legs in overalls sticking out from underneath it. The car looked like it belonged to a scarecrow, as it was covered with straw and dust.

At the vicarage, there was a scarecrow relaxing in a garden chair. His legs were crossed and there was a large straw hat covering his face. A fork was upright in the ground next to him, and there was also an empty mug.

"Someone's been working hard!" chuckled Farmer Green.
"I think it's supposed to be the vicar," said Sally, pointing to the black and white collar around the scarecrow's neck.

Parked in the driveway of the house on the corner was a vintage motorcycle, being ridden by a scarecrow biker. She was wearing a leather jacket, jeans, big motorcycle boots, and a crash helmet. Long strands of straw stuck out from under the helmet, looking like long fair hair.

"Wow! You can hardly see the scarecrow under all that!" exclaimed Sally.

They looked up at the big house on the corner where the old phone booth was. There was a burglar in a mask and a striped sweater, climbing out from one of the upstairs windows. He had a sack marked "swag" on his back. The sack had all sorts of interesting lumps and bumps, as if it were filled with things he had stolen.

In the school playground, there were lots of small scarecrows. All the children had made one and they were having their own “Scarecrow Music Festival”. There was a scarecrow band on the stage, and it looked as if the other scarecrows were dancing. Behind them, the shapes of lots of brightly patterned cardboard tents could be seen.

In the band, one scarecrow was playing the guitar, one sat at a huge drum kit, and one in a red wig was singing into a microphone. The drum kit had the name of the band painted on it: The Scaredy Crows. “I hope they sound better than they look!” whispered Farmer Green to Sally.

"The scarecrows are fantastic," said Sally. "Everyone has tried really hard."

On the village green, under the noticeboard, was another tent, a real one this time. Outside the tent was a pretend campfire with red and yellow flames made from paper. A scarecrow camper was cooking cardboard sausages. A small scarecrow dog sat next to him, looking at the sausages.

In the garden of Doctor Crisp's cottage, there was a fisherman scarecrow. He was sitting on a stool and fishing in the pond. There was a bucket with some plastic fish in it and Doctor Crisp's fishing tackle box on the ground.

"Look at all those hooks and floats and flies and things," said Sally.

Next, they strolled along Duck Lane. “I always love walking down here,” said Sally, “with all the trees and the lovely dappled light. According to the map, there are eight more scarecrows along here.”

At Willow Cottage, there was a photographer scarecrow poised to take their photo as they walked by. A big handwritten notice said “Smile!”

The next scarecrow was sitting in an old tub, with a shower sticking up and over it. White, fleecy, pretend bubbles covered the top of the tub and the scarecrow's head, arms, and feet were sticking out of it.

The scarecrow was wearing a flowery shower cap and scrubbing its back with a huge loofah on a stick.

“Woah!” screamed Sally, as they turned the corner and she almost crashed into a phantom scarecrow hanging from a tree. The phantom scarecrow was covered with a white sheet, with two holes for eyes cut out of it.

“That gave me a real fright too!” cried Farmer Green.

When they got back to the village hall, they sat down to enjoy a cup of tea and some cake. Sally chose lemon drizzle cake and Farmer Green chose a slice of gingerbread.

“I think that is the biggest number of scarecrows there has ever been,” said Farmer Green.
“It’s been the best scarecrow festival we have ever had,” added Sally.

Everyone was supposed to vote for the scarecrow they liked the best. The prize was a meal in the local restaurant. The winner would be announced at the end of the weekend when all of the votes had been counted. On their way out, Sally and Farmer Green put their votes in the box.

Which scarecrow would you vote for?